Pick
Your Own
Quest

Series by Connor Hoover

Camp Hercules
Wizards of Tomorrow
Alien Treasure Hunters
Pick Your Own Quest

Pick Your Own Quest

ESCAPE FROM MINECRAFT

by
CONNOR HOOVER

Pick Your Own Quest:
Escape From Minecraft

Paperback ISBN: 978-1717505224

For Video Game Players
everywhere!

Finally! Your homework is done. Okay, sure, you could have spent a little more time on reading, but you can't find anything good to read. Dad's making dinner. Mom's still not home. Now is the perfect time to sneak in a little bit of Minecraft!

You load up the game and you can't believe it when you see that the Most Epic Excellent Survival server isn't full! Finally! You've waited forever to try out this server. You log on . . .

If you dare, turn the page.

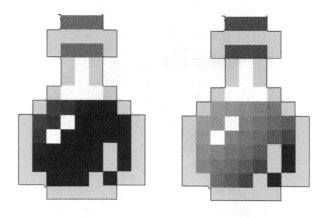

etting onto the server is perfect! Except why did it have to happen when you only have like ten minutes to play before dinner? Still, this will be the best ten minutes of your life!

Even though there are other people on the server, you don't see anyone else. You walk forward into the first building you see. There's some weird sign outside the door. It says: NEVER DRINK THE GREEN POTION. How cool is that!

You open the door and walk inside. Torches line the walls. Ahead of you are two chests. In one chest is a yellow potion. In the other is a green potion. You remember the sign on the door, warning you not to drink the green potion. That's ridiculous. You drink the green potion.

Everything goes black. Not just on the screen, but all around you. When the light slowly returns, you look around. You aren't in your bedroom anymore. You are in some kind of room lit with torches. There are two chests in the room. The weird thing is that everything looks really blocky. It's almost like . . .

No, that can't be right. You close your eyes, hoping you're wrong, but when you open them again, nothing has changed. You are inside Minecraft! It was the green potion! Somehow it brought you inside the game. Maybe drinking the yellow potion will take you back out of the game.

If you drink the yellow potion, turn to page 4.

If you think drinking any more potion is a really bad idea and decide to explore instead, turn to page 6.

If there is a way for you to get back to the real world, then that has to be your top priority. And the potion is sure to be the answer. You open the chest and drink the yellow potion. It tastes awful! Almost like . . . sour lemonade. That's gross.

You toss the empty potion bottle over your head. The glass smashes on the ground, and a huge cloud of yellow smoke comes out. It fills the room and is so thick that you can't see a thing. You hold your breath and look for the door, but you can't find it. Finally, you can't hold your breath any longer, and you breathe in.

The air tastes just as bad as the potion, but it doesn't kill you, so you consider that a win. Finally, after what feels like forever, the smoke clears. But wait, the door is gone and there is no sign of the two chests. You realize that you aren't in the building anymore. Instead, you're in the middle of a swamp. Maybe a witch left the potions for you.

In every direction is swamp water and vines and plants. You spot something up ahead, and you hurry toward it. It's a witch's hut. She could be home, and that could end up really bad. But what if she's the witch who made the potions? Something inside could help you get home. You have to try.

4

You creep up the steps of the witch's hut. You think about turning around and running, but you're not a coward (or at least you're trying not to be). You take a deep breath and open the door.

The hut is empty. There's a fire in the fireplace, but there is no witch inside. Things are definitely going your way.

The witch has a bunch of food, and you stock up on it so you don't run out later. The apples are all a little shriveled, and you skip the gross things like pig's hooves and spider webs (because who would eat that junk), but you take as much as you can carry.

On the other side of the room from the food chests is the nicest brewing stand you've ever seen in your life. There are about a million different ingredients on shelves and there's also an entire chest filled with pre-made potions. One of these potions could be what you're looking for. But you have no idea what these potions do because none of them are labeled.

Turn to page 8.

You ou leave the room and wind up outside. The sun is straight overhead, so you don't need to worry about monsters. You can't find anywhere that looks like it would take you back to the real world, and anyway, how often do you get a chance like this? You bet none of your friends have ever been trapped inside Minecraft. You should definitely explore. Time passes differently inside Minecraft anyway. You have lots of time.

It looks like there are tons of mountains off to the left with a bunch of trees around. Things are also moving. They look like cows. Or maybe villagers. Even though they aren't real people, they might know the way out. Also, mountains mean mines! But over to the right is a desert. Something tells you there might be a river near the desert. And if you build a boat and float down the river, you'd be able to see a lot more of this world. Still, you hate sand. It gets everywhere and makes you itch.

You turn your back on the desert and head for the mountains. You aren't far when a wolf runs up to you. You don't see any more wolves, but being eaten by a wolf pack doesn't sound so fun. You check your inventory, and you have a bone! The wolf takes the bone and immediately becomes your best friend and wolf companion! You name him Lucky. He runs forward and you follow him. You thought he was supposed to follow you, but maybe the rules are a little different when you're actually inside Minecraft.

You're halfway up the mountain when you see a tunnel. It's still daytime, so there's plenty of time, but you also don't want to go mining when you're totally unprepared. While you're standing there trying to decide what to do, Lucky barks one time and runs down into the tunnel! It's horrible! Sure, you've only known him for a few minutes, but you got really attached. He needs you, and if there are monsters in the tunnel, he could get killed. Of course, so could you.

If you go into the tunnel after Lucky, turn to page 12.

It's not going to help Lucky if you die, too. If you decide to gather supplies instead, turn to page 10.

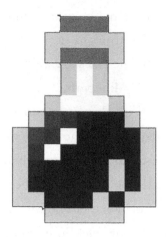

There are potions of every single color and size, and you grab as many as you can. She even has four different shades of green potions. Green potion is what got you into this mess in the first place. Since the yellow potion didn't take you back to the real world, maybe the green will. But you can try it later. Right now, you need to finish getting the potions and get out.

The witch has a pretty nice helmet also, so you take that, because maybe it will give you some kind of special powers. It's her only one, so she's bound to miss it, but she's not here. After you've taken everything you can hold, you leave the hut.

The top step makes a horrible sound when you step on it, and a cloud of smoke billows off the ground. When it vanishes, the witch is there! This is horrible. She's going to kill you. And there's nowhere for you to run. But all she does is smile.

Sure, her smile is kinda gross. She's missing a ton of teeth, and what teeth she does have are yellow and black. She definitely should have flossed and brushed when she was younger. It makes you want to brush your teeth the next chance you get.

She glances at the helmet you're carrying. She knows you've taken her stuff. You open your mouth to start making excuses, but she says, "Don't worry. I can help you get back to your world."

She knows what happened to you! She must be responsible. If she really can help you, then that is perfect. Still, she doesn't look very trust-worthy.

If you take help from the witch, turn to page 16.

If you tell her 'no thanks' and that you don't want her help, turn to page 14.

Getting some supplies is really important. You start by breaking some trees. You manage to find some apples. You eat a couple because you're hungry. It's weird, because even though you're here in the video game, they fill you up! You accidentally drop your pickaxe on your foot, and it hurts! It's like everything that is happening inside the game is really happening to you.

Wait. Does that mean if you die in the game, then you're really going to die? No, that's silly. It's just a video game. Or is it?

You see a village in the distance, and you really miss Lucky, so it would be nice to find other people. But the sun is getting low in the sky. Maybe you should build a house first to spend the night in.

If you hurry to the village, because there will be people and shelter there, turn to page 18.

If you build yourself a house and bed, turn to page 20.

The tunnel looks horrible, all dark and scary, but you have to find Lucky! What if something eats him? And it can't just be coincidence that he came up to you. He could even know the way out of Minecraft when you're ready to leave. You take a deep breath and set off into the tunnel.

You're only two steps in and the walls seem to close in around you. It's so much worse than when you're playing on your computer at home. It's dark and the walls are wet and there are all sorts of freaky noises.

You walk straight for a while because there is only one way to go, but soon you come to a fork in the tunnel. There are two paths. One leads up and one leads down. In the tunnel that leads down, there is light, far ahead, and light is good. It will keep monsters away. But there is an amazing smell coming from the tunnel that leads up, almost like something is cooking. It makes your stomach grumble. And Lucky may have headed for the smell. Of course, he might have headed for the light, too.

If you take the path down, toward the light, turn to page 22.

If you trust your stomach and take the path up, toward the smell, turn to page 24.

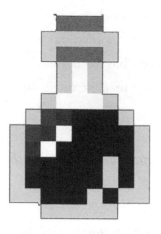

You would be seriously crazy to let this old hag witch help you. Everyone knows that witches can't be trusted. You learned that the first day you played Minecraft. Trust the witch! It's funny how ridiculous the thought is. Still, you don't want to upset her.

You tell her 'No thank you' as politely as you possibly can, and you try to scoot around her because what you do need to do is get out of here. When she hears your answer, the smile slides from her face and a giant wrinkly frown appears.

"No one says no to me!" she shrieks, and she lunges at you with her long fingernails extended.

14

You jump back and grab the first potion you can get your hands on, and you throw it at her. You think it's purple, but you don't take the time to look. The second the potion hits the witch, she starts to melt, and she melts into a giant pool of goop right there on the porch of her hut.

Well, that was easy. You set out on your way, leaving the witch hut far behind. You're back in the swamp when the sun starts to set, and instantly, a zombie appears. It's coming right for you.

If you run away from the zombie, turn to page 26.

If you throw a potion at the zombie, turn to page 59.

You would be silly not to take help from the witch. After all you are trapped inside a video game, for real, and you have no idea how to get out. And she may have been involved in getting you here.

"Thank you so much," you say. "I would love help. I want to get back to the real world."

She gives you her gross smile again and cackles a little. And then she shows you her Nether portal.

That's it! A Nether portal is the perfect way to get back. You can go to the Nether and find a portal back to your world. She tells you that she would be happy to let you use the portal if you go into it, gather some

Nether Wart for her, and bring it back. After that, you will be free to use the Nether portal anytime you want. This sounds like a pretty sweet deal. Except the Nether is a dangerous place.

You ask her if she has any weapons, and she tells you that her only weapons are potions. Potions won't be much good against monsters.

If you go off in search of weapons before going through the Nether portal, turn to page 28.

If you take your chances and go into the Nether portal, turn to page 60.

You stop collecting wood and head for the village. If you hurry, you'll get there before the sun goes down. But the terrain is a lot rougher than you thought, and you have to go way out of your way to get there. You almost fall off the side of a mountain, but you catch yourself at the last minute.

Once you're back on the right path, you realize your stomach hurts. OMG you're almost out of food! You eat the last couple apples you have, but it's not going to be enough. There are some trees off to the left, and you grab a few more apples from them. But it's getting really dark, really fast. If you don't do something immediately, you aren't going to make it.

If you run for the village, as fast as you can, turn to page 61.

If you quick build yourself a shelter and try to survive the night, turn to page 70.

You find some sheep, and collect some wool. You think about all the fun colors you could dye their wool, but there's no time for that right now. Tomorrow maybe you'll do that. Right now, you make a bed. And then you build a small room around it. There's no time to do anything fancy. The sun is getting really low in the sky. You want to make a door, but that will have to wait. Instead, you put the final block on your house just before the monsters come. You are safe!

You sleep through the night. It's the best night of sleep you've ever had in a video game. Okay, fine, it's the only night of sleep you've ever had in a video game.

You wonder how time is passing out in the real world. Has anyone in your family noticed that you're gone? If you stay here forever, will they miss you? Or what if they unplug your computer? That would kill your connection to the server. You hope that doesn't happen.

In the morning, you walk outside, and the first thing you do is make a tall tower so you'll be able to spot your house from far away. The tower is pretty cool, and it makes you kind of want to work on your house some more. But the village isn't that far, and you did want to check it out. The villagers could be your friends.

If you work on your house for a while, turn to page 30.

If you lock your house and head for the village, turn to page 32.

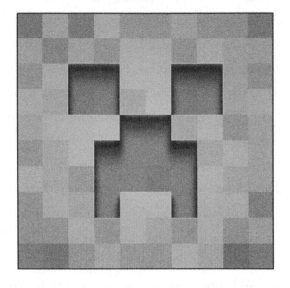

You can't let your stomach make the decisions around here. You take the tunnel that heads down, toward the light. You walk for what feels like forever, but you don't want to run, because it's still kind of dark, and what if you fall into a bottomless pit or something? That would be horrible. Wait! What if that happened to Lucky?

No, you have to believe he is alive. You keep going and finally you reach the light. There are four people standing in the center of a circle of torches. They immediately look your way when you come into the room.

"I lost my dog Lucky. Have you seen him?" you ask, because you aren't sure if they're friendly, and everyone loves dogs, so this might help them like you.

They haven't seen your dog, but they do seem really friendly, and they invite you to join their group. You aren't sure if they're NPCs or other players on the server, but if you ask them, they're going to think you're crazy, so you keep your mouth shut.

They tell you they are about to go on a monster hunt. Legend has it that there is a skeleton that roams these tunnels with full gold armor. Full gold armor! You've always dreamed of owning a set of full gold armor. But you still need to find Lucky. You can't get distracted by a monster hunt.

If you join them and go on the monster hunt, turn to page 34.

If you tell them no thanks and leave them, turn to page 36.

You trust your stomach and you follow the smell. It's almost like bacon cooking. Maybe they have bacon when you're actually inside Minecraft. And if Lucky had smelled bacon, then that's totally the direction he would have gone. Bacon is amazing. The path leads up. It's a lot harder to walk uphill inside Minecraft than when you're playing at home. Pretty soon, you are out of breath, and you have to stop and take breaks. But you continue on. You will find Lucky.

Lava flows around you, and the scent gets stronger. And maybe it doesn't smell so much like bacon, but it still smells pretty good. Finally the path flattens out, and you see an entryway ahead. It looks like shadows inside, which could mean Lucky. You go in.

There is no sign of Lucky, but there are a bunch of people. You tell them everything, about how you were playing the game, got onto the server, and ended up here. And they tell you that the exact same thing happened to them.

This is not the best news. This means that you could be stuck here like them. They notice you're kind of sad, so they tell you about their plan to return to the real world. It involved sacrifices to the volcano.

You aren't sure about sacrifices. That doesn't sound very good, but if it can really get you out of this server, then maybe it's your only choice. And you kind of do want bacon.

If you ask to join them on their quest to get back to the real world, turn to page 62.

If you tell them no thanks and leave them, turn to page 38.

25

You are not messing around with a zombie. And everyone knows that potions and zombies are not a good match. You probably would have died if you'd thrown a potion at him. But luckily you didn't.

You pick up the pace, because it's getting darker every second, and monster noises are all around you. You find a small island in the swamp that's big enough for a shelter, build a shelter, and sleep. In the morning, the monsters are gone.

You keep going, and the swamp gives way to a lake. There's a boat waiting for you. Except that's kind of weird. It could be a trap.

If you get the boat, because there are no monsters on boats, turn to page 40.

If you don't get in the boat, turn to page 64.

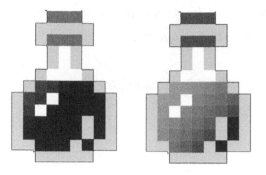

You tell the witch that you're going to find some weapons and then will be back.

"You better," she says. "Or bad luck will haunt you forever."

That sounds horrible, so you promise her you will return. Then she tells you about a village that's not too far away. They have a blacksmith shop there. Then you set out through the swamp toward the village.

It's getting dark, so you make a shelter and sleep before continuing on, but then first thing in the morning, you find the village. It is exactly where the witch said it would be. And the blacksmith villager has to be the nicest person you've ever met. He gives you so many weapons that you have to pick and choose because you can't carry them all. Then he asks you why you want them.

You tell him about the witch and the Nether portal and how you just want to return to the real world. But the blacksmith tells you that you can't trust the witch. He says that she will never let you leave.

If you return to the witch because you promised, turn to page 42.

If you take his advice and do not return to the witch, turn to page 44.

You are going to have the coolest house in the history of Minecraft, because things look so much more awesome here inside the game. If only your friends could see it. You start by collecting some materials and making a basement and a second floor. A glass ceiling looks really cool, so you do that next.

You head outside to get some plants, and there are animals all around. You tame some chickens and sheep and build a fence to keep them in. The chickens have a baby, and you decide to make their pen even bigger. They seem to really like you.

In your mind, you imagine building a barn and a playground and all sorts of things. And building is so much easier when you're actually inside the game. Maybe you could even build an amusement park! That would be amazing!

There's a noise behind you. There are some horses not too far away. And wait! Is that a giraffe? You didn't even know there were giraffes in Minecraft. Maybe you could build a zoo.

If you decide to build your own amusement park, turn to page 46.

If you think the animals would really love to be part of a zoo, turn to page 66.

You head for the village. The sun is nice and bright in the morning sky and the path is rough. It's a really good thing you waited until morning to come this way. In the dark, this path could be deadly. You reach the village before the sun is even halfway up the sky.

There's a fence outside, but a sign says, WELCOME TRAVELERS! You take that as an invitation and walk inside. Most of the villagers hardly look your way. They seem to be busy doing day-to-day stuff. One women runs a food cart and you hurry over and trade with her to get some bread. She says she baked it fresh this morning. That's another good reason you waited until morning. The bread last night would have been stale.

You walk through the town square. There's a library. Lots of houses. Maybe a town hall. Out front of town hall is another sign. It says, JOB OPENING. KING. NO EXPERIENCE NEEDED. Being king of the village would be pretty cool. Your house was nice and all, but this whole place could be your kingdom.

While you're looking at the sign, an old villager walks up to you.

"I'm Crazy Joe," he says. "And I know where you can find 500 diamonds."

500 diamonds! Is he kidding? You've played a lot (and I mean A LOT) of Minecraft, but you've never found anywhere near that many diamonds.

If you ask him where the diamonds are, turn to page 68.

If you forget about the diamonds and take the job of king instead, turn to page 48.

You tell the four people that you'll join the hunt! There's a bunch of celebrating. You all eat and drink to make sure you build up your strength. Then they help you craft some amazing weapons so you'll be prepared for whatever you come across in the tunnels. You all get a good night sleep, inside the circle of torches. In the morning, you are ready to go.

You set out, down the tunnel. The tunnels all look the same to you, but the people seem to know where they are going, almost like they've been this way before. You fight all sorts of other monsters, including skeletons, but there is no sign of a skeleton in full gold armor. But you and your new friends are not going to give up.

Something catches your eye. Something shiny. You turn and see what has to be the skeleton in gold armor. You run after it, because your friends are going to think you're really awesome if you find it first. But when you get to the place where you saw it, there is no sign of it. It must've gone on ahead.

If you run back to your friends and tell them, because you don't want to get too far away from them, turn to page 71.

If you keep going on your own because you are going to be the one to find it, turn to page 50.

You don't have time for a monster hunt. And there is no such thing as a skeleton wearing full gold armor. It's ridiculous. What you need to do is find Lucky, explore some more, and find a way out of the Minecraft world. You tell the four people 'No thanks,' and you set off on your own, leaving them to their monster hunt. They wish you good luck and head their own way.

You mine as you go, following the tunnels and making marks so you'll remember which way you went. You stop to eat. You sleep. You do not give up. And finally, you think you hear Lucky ahead. It sounds like some kind of barking. It almost sounds like . . . like he's stuck behind a wall.

You mine to open the wall, because you have to find Lucky. But when you open the wall, there's no sign of him. He must be ahead. You step into the opening, and fall into a ravine. Thankfully, it's not too deep, and you don't die. It's also kind of cool. Even from where you sit on the ground, you see gems sparkling in the lava light.

If you decide to mine in the ravine for a little bit, turn to page 72.

If getting out is your top priority, turn to page 54.

You don't want anything to do with sacrifices. You smile and thank the people for their wonderful invitation to join them, and then you get out of there as fast as you can. They are crazy. You're sure of it. You look back about fifty different times, but they aren't following. They don't want to leave the volcano since they think it's the way out.

You continue forward, and before you know it, you see light ahead. But it's not torch light. It is the sun. You come out of the tunnel, up near the top of a mountain. Well, actually it's the same volcano the crazy people were sacrificing to. Lava flows down the sides everywhere. But you're on a nice platform, and there on the platform is Lucky!

38

He runs to you, and you guys have the best reunion ever. You hug him and tell him never to run off again, and he licks you. It's great.

Now that you've found him, you two need to get down the volcano. The outside is covered with lava though, so it's going to be really dangerous. But it's not like the inside was much better. The crazy people are back that way, not to mention monsters of all kinds.

If you go down the side of the volcano, turn to page 52.

If you go back inside the tunnel, and go that way, turn to page 73.

The boat is a good sign, and you hop aboard. You name it the S.S. EL DORADO because it sounds really cool, and you'd love to find a city of gold some day. You toy with the idea of living in Minecraft forever and building your own city of gold but decide against it. You can always do that once you're back in the real world.

The boat takes you far away from the swamp, across the lake, and to an ocean. It's weird how you can even smell the salt water. And you can fish. There are tons of fish around. As you're looking down you see an underwater temple. Temples are magical places, and there could be a way out inside the temple.

40

You put on the helmet that you stole from the witch, and you dive down to check it out. The helmet seems to let you breathe underwater. There are guardians everywhere. Like so many more than when you're just playing back in the real world. They come at you from all sides, and you aren't sure you can fight them off.

If you swim back to the surface, turn to page 74.

If you fight the guardians, turn to page 56.

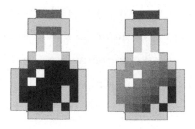

Even though the blacksmith told you that the witch can't be trusted, you have to return. You promised her that you would, and if you don't keep your promise, it doesn't make you a very nice person. You thank him for his advice and return to the witch hut.

The witch is overjoyed to see you. She cackles and smiles. She tells you that she didn't think you would come back, but that because you did, there will be great rewards. The only reward you want is to get home.

She has you drink a potion that will make you extra strong and then sends you through the Nether portal to get her Nether Wart. After the world settles, the monsters start coming. You fight zombie pigmen and wither skeletons, but against your weapons and the potion, nothing stands a chance. You defeat everything that comes your way.

As you're fighting a zombie pigman, you spot some soul sand. That is where the witch's Nether Wart will be. You defeat the zombie pigman and run for the soul sand, and you easily collect the Nether Wart. But then you look forward and spot another portal. This could be the portal back to the real world. Maybe you should go through it. But you promised the witch you would return. As you're trying to decide, you look again at the soul sand. The screaming faces are really creepy up close. They almost scream at you to set them free. You wonder if one of the potions that you have could set them free. Maybe they could help you.

If you go through the portal without returning to the witch, turn to page 80.

If you go back to the witch to give her the Nether Wart, turn to page 75.

If you try to set the faces trapped in the soul sand free, turn to page 106.

No way are you going back to that witch. If the villagers tell you that she can't be trusted, then you are going to believe them. You thank them and promise to write an amazing story about them when you get back to the real world. They are so grateful that they give you a diamond pickaxe as thanks. You almost tell them that it is too nice of a gift to accept, except you really want it, so you just say, "Thank you."

You spend the next few days with them, planning out the best place to get the materials to make your own Nether portal. You may not be able to use the witch's portal, but that doesn't mean you can't build your own. After a lot of careful planning on exactly what you need to do, you set out.

The villagers have told you the best and closest place to find lava, and you head toward it. But on the way, you spot something shiny. And shiny could mean gold. You've always loved gold. And if you can see it from this far away, maybe it's even an entire city made of gold, like El Dorado, the golden city from legends.

If you keep going toward the lava, turn to page 76.

If you head toward the shiny object instead, turn to page 57.

Your amusement park is going to be epic! You make sure you have plenty of food and wood for torches, and you head into the mines. Sure, you collect lots of cool gems, but what you're really looking for is redstone. You've spent half the day mining, when you finally hit the mother lode. There is so much redstone, that it takes you two days to mine it all, making trips back and forth to your house to store it in your chests.

When you finally think you have enough, you start on your amusement park. You build a slide, which is fun, but good amusement parks have more than slides. You make some food stands, because when villagers come to your park, they're going to be hungry. Maybe they'll pay you in emeralds. After that, you make a haunted house where you trap some monsters. The monsters aren't so happy about it, but that's too bad. They would kill you if they had a chance.

46

The haunted house is really cool, but now it's time to use the redstone. You make a train track that goes around the entire park. But what you really want next is something up high. A roller coaster would be awesome. You went on one back in the real world last summer and loved it. Or maybe a giant trampoline like your neighbors have. Mom never lets you use it. She says trampolines are dangerous.

If you build the roller coaster next, turn to page 78.

If you build a trampoline, turn to page 86.

Diamonds are cool and all, but it's not every day that you can be a real life king. You go inside town hall, apply for the job, and they immediately put a crown on your head. You walk outside and all the villagers bow to you. You are their new king!

You start by building a castle, and you build a tall wall around the entire kingdom to protect it. After all, these are your villagers, and it is your responsibility to protect them. They could die without your protection. Once the wall is done, you start on the throne room. This is where villagers will be able to come talk to you. It has to look perfect.

You're almost done when you realize that your throne would look so much better if it were covered completely in emeralds. You go to your villagers and ask them for emeralds.

They say no.

If you try to forcibly take the emeralds from the villagers, turn to page 81.

Emeralds aren't everything. If you focus on being a good king instead, turn to page 98.

You got this on your own. You will find that skeleton with the full gold armor, you'll kill it, and then you will show your friends. They'll think you are the best monster hunter ever! You stay super quiet and you listen for the skeleton. There are a couple paths to choose from, but you're sure you hear it coming from the tunnel on the right. You creep down the tunnel, and when you turn the corner, there it is!

You're so excited, you almost panic, but then you remember your mission. This is what you've been searching for. The legend is true. The skeleton is really real. You take a deep breath, prepare your weapons, and then you kill it. The armor falls to the ground and you collect it immediately. And then you decide to try it on, because it is gold armor. Everyone wants gold armor.

The second it is on, you feel more powerful than ever before. You feel like you could defeat any monster that comes your way. But enough is enough. It's time to take it back and show your friends. Of course, then you're going to have to share it with them, and now that it's on, you kind of want to keep it all for yourself.

If you head back to your friends, because you never would have known about the gold armor if not for them, turn to page 82.

If you decide to keep it for yourself and head far away from your friends, turn to page 58.

You are not going back inside that volcano. There are about five hundred things that can kill you that way. You and Lucky start down the side of the mountain, making sure to stay far away from the flows of lava. There are rocks, and you jump from one to the next, making your path. Lucky follows easily. He's a lot more nimble than you.

You trip and almost die a few times, but you don't. You are a survivor. Oh, except night is coming. You build a quick shelter there on the side of the mountain, and Lucky protects you through the night. You aren't sure what you would do without him. As you try to sleep you think of all the things you miss. Popcorn. Hamburgers. Even broccoli. Okay, not broccoli. You don't miss broccoli.

In the morning, you wake up and Lucky has found you a hamburger! You have no idea how. You didn't even know that was possible. He is the best dog in the entire world, and you can't imagine ever leaving him. But you do want to get home. He brings you some popcorn next, almost like he knows what you're thinking.

If you stay with Lucky in Minecraft forever, turn to page 96.

If you have to find a way home, turn to page 90.

Forget mining. You need to get out of this ravine. Ravines are scary places with monsters
and lava and so many things that can kill you.
You've played enough Minecraft to know this. You're
not stupid.

You take your time looking around, trying to figure
the best way out of this ravine. Water and lava flow
freely, but there is enough rock to build a solid staircase.
It looks like the best place for the staircase is on the
other side of the ravine from the lava. Lava is tricky,
and it's best to stay away from it. You start building your
staircase.

You build it out of the rocks around you, making
sure it is plenty wide so you don't fall off. A 1x1 staircase may be fine when you're playing the game at home,

but here, inside Minecraft, it seems too small. So it takes you longer than you planned, but better to be safe than dead. You climb as you build.

At the next level you build, you find a tunnel! Oh wait, you find two tunnels. One leads off to the left and one leads off to the right.

If you take the tunnel on the left, turn to page 84.

If you take the tunnel on the right, turn to page 94.

Sure, there are a ton of guardians, but you are an expert Minecraft fighter. You fight one after another after another. They keep coming, and you keep fighting. You push your way into the underwater temple. You take cover in air bubbles when you need to, but you fight the guardians until they are all gone.

Oh, yeah, but then there's the elder guardian and he is mega-powerful. He almost kills you five times. But you keep at it. No way are you going to die. Finally, you defeat him! As he falls to the ground, you notice there is an airtight room behind him, almost like he was protecting it. But it could be a dungeon, and if you go in, there might not be a way to get back out. Still, you feel like you should check it out.

If you go into the airtight room, turn to page 100.

If you look around the underwater temple some more, turn to page 105.

S hiny definitely means gold, and you have time to check this out before building your Nether portal. You head toward whatever is making such a beautiful light.

It takes you a lot longer to reach the object than you thought. You have to climb halfway up the side of a mountain. But when you get there, you can't believe what you see. It's a statue of you made entirely out of gold. If, for a second, you thought it wasn't you, there are signs all around with your name on them. There is no mistaking it.

Okay, so this is a little bit creepy. You aren't going to lie. A statue of you? Like who built that? You really want to know, but also, it's kind of super weird and maybe a little scary.

If you investigate a little bit longer, turn to page 92.

If you get out of there as fast as you can, turn to page 102.

Y ou worked really hard for this gold armor. There is no way you are going back to share it with your friends. And it's not like they're really your friends. You've only known them for a few hours. They'll forget all about you and can keep searching for the skeleton in the gold armor on their own. Maybe there are two of them. You doubt it, but that's not really your problem.

You head the complete opposite direction of the way they were but you're going to need to get some supplies to live. And almost like the game is justifying your decision, you come across an underground bunker. It is stocked full of supplies! You can live here forever. And your friends will never find you here, and you can keep the gold armor forever.

But wait . . . if you stay here forever, you will never find Lucky, and you will never find a way back to the real world.

If you take the safe route, and stay in the underground bunker forever, turn to page 88.

If you leave the bunker and keep looking for a way out, turn to page 104.

You've fought zombies a million times before. This one is no different. And you just killed a witch with the potion. That must be why the witch has so many potions. She must use them to defend herself.

You grab another purple potion from your bag and you throw it at the zombie. But the zombie's strength increases. How is that even possible? It killed the witch. Oh wait . . .

You remember something about potions and zombies. Like maybe potions can help them instead of kill them. The zombie hits you and you fall over into the swamp. As you sink down into the swamp water, you wish you'd remembered this little detail earlier. It's your last thought as the swamp water covers you.

THE END

You tell the witch that you are going into the Nether. You will find her Nether Wart, bring it back to her, and then find a portal to your world.

The world goes all woozy as you go through the portal, but it's not unexpected. You've been to the Nether lots of times before. But you've never been in real life. It's totally different. There are monsters everywhere.

You reach for a weapon and remember that you don't have any. You need to get out of here and come back when you're prepared. Except, wait! Is that an EXIT sign ahead? Like exit back to the real world? It has to be. You run for it. You're going to make it. You almost have a foot through the opening. But right before you do, a ghast shoots you and you die.

THE END

Y ou run as fast as you can, straight toward the village. There are a couple of places you have to jump, and you fall off a small hill, but it doesn't kill you. The village is getting closer. Lights are on. The torches will keep the monsters away. You keep running. The villagers all turn toward you, like they're happy you are coming. There's a sign out front, but you don't take the time to read it. When you get close enough to the people, you see that they're zombies! They're going to kill you. You turn back to the sign. It says: BEWARE. VILLAGERS TURN INTO ZOMBIES AT NIGHT. You should have taken the time to read it earlier.

You dash around the villagers, because your survival instinct is kicking in. They almost let you through. There's a building ahead. You run in and the door slams closed behind you. You're going to be okay.

You can't believe how fast your heart is beating. But those zombies had been scary. From outside, you hear them moaning. They're getting closer. You back up, toward the wall, and then you remember that thing about zombies. You'd been in such a hurry that you forgot.

They break down the door and kill you.

THE END

61

Y ou don't care how these people do it, if they can get back to the real world, then you are going to join them. They are thrilled, and you all celebrate with a huge meal. There is bacon, just like you thought. Then, after you are all full, they show you a room where they trap and keep monsters.

The people tell you about their great plan to get back to the real world. Every day they throw a monster into the volcano as a sacrifice. They are convinced the volcano is alive and will somehow send them back to the real world as thanks.

This is the stupidest, craziest idea you've ever heard in your life, and you tell them so. Like who in their right mind would think this? That's when you realize that these people are not in their right minds. They've been trapped in the server for too long.

You turn to run, because you need to get out of here, but you aren't moving so fast because you ate so much bacon, and the people grab you. They drag you over to the top of the volcano.

"This will be our best sacrifice yet," one of them says.

Then they throw you in. As you fall, you can't help but wonder if they are right. Maybe you, as a sacrifice, will get them all back to the real world. But you hope not.

THE END

No way are you getting into the boat. The boat is totally a trap. Like who leaves a perfect boat all alone? Someone who wants to kill you, that's who. You walk about from the boat and keep going through the swamp.

You see mountains in the distance. Maybe you can find some villagers near the mountains. Or maybe there's a way out, though you have no idea what it might be. You don't want to be stuck in this game forever.

You sit down to rest for a little while and have a snack, when suddenly you are swarmed by slimes. They're kind of cute at first, almost like little jumpy blobs. You back up away from them, but they are behind you also. Then they jump on you over and over again until you die.

THE END

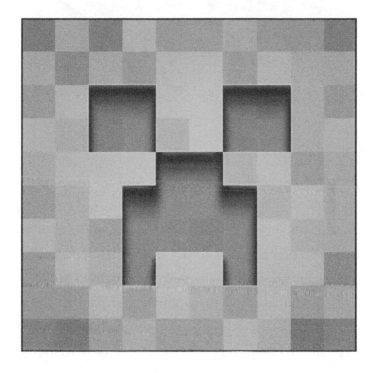

The animals need you. You promise them you'll be right back, then you head for the horses and giraffes. They are super easy to tame, and they follow you back to your house. You map out a huge area and make them each pens. They walk right in, and you feed them apples to make them happy. It doesn't stop with giraffes though. Next you find elephants. And two hippopotamuses. There are animals everywhere.

Soon your zoo is better than any zoo you've ever been to in your life. And the animals are all so happy. You pass the next few days collecting animals and food, and you go from pen to pen feeding them and taking of them. You've never felt so happy in your life. You don't think it could ever get any better. Except then Lucky runs up to you, wagging his tail! You can't believe it. He found you! You vow to never leave him again, and you find him a mate. They have a cute little wolf baby.

Once your zoo is perfect, you let the villagers know about it. They tell other villages. People come from all over to visit your zoo. This is the perfect life. You decide to stay here forever and take care of your animals. Every so often you miss the real world, but you have everything you need right here in Minecraft.

THE END

You immediately ask this Crazy Joe guy where the diamonds are. He tells you about a cave that no one can find. You ask him how he knows and why he doesn't go get the diamonds himself, and he explains that he has a rare allergy to diamonds and can't go anywhere near them. It's a pretty good reason to stay away from diamonds. Luckily you do not have the same allergy.

You head to the cave, leaving the village behind. Once you find the diamonds, you can always return and become king then. And with 500 diamonds, people will be really impressed.

The cave is exactly where Crazy Joe said it would be. You light a torch and go inside. He told you to go to the end of the cave, turning right whenever you have a choice. You do this and finally come to a perfectly square room. It's huge, and in the room are the diamonds! You don't count them, but there are enough diamonds here to build a castle out of. Maybe even way more than 500.

You start collecting them. You're so busy with the diamonds, that you don't notice the spawner on the side of the room. Cave spiders appear out of nowhere, and they aren't happy that you are in their cave. They don't care about diamonds. All they care about is poisoning you, which they do.

THE END

Y ou know exactly what you are doing, and you construct your shelter super-fast. It may be small, but no monsters will be able to break in. You sit in the dark, inside, listening to all the monsters roam around outside. They smell you, but they can't get to you. You miss Lucky. Maybe you should have followed him into the tunnel instead. When morning comes, you vow to go back and find him.

You start to doze off, because you're sure you've been sitting in here for hours, but a horrible pain wakes you up. It's your stomach. You are starving. You check your inventory, but you don't have any apples left. This is the worst! You're about to break your shelter, but then you hear a monster right outside. It will kill you. Still you have to do it. But as much as you know this, you can't bring yourself to face the monster. Instead, you slowly starve to death.

THE END

Y ou run back down the tunnel they way you came. You are going to get your friends, tell them that you're sure you saw the skeleton in the gold armor, and then you can all go together to hunt it. You stumble on a rock and fall, but get right back up and keep going. The tunnel is taking way longer than you remember. But your friends are up ahead. You see the light of their torches. But you don't have any light, and you keep running into things on your way.

Every time you run into something, you yell and make all sorts of noise. You're making so much noise, in fact, that your friends have no idea that it's you running down the tunnel toward them. They think you're a monster. And as soon as they have a clear shot, they shoot you with arrows.

THE END

How often to you get the chance to mine in a ravine, in real life!? Well, at least as real life as this entire thing seems to be. It sure feels real. The lava makes the air hot around you. The gems are sparkling, ready for you to collect them. The water tastes refreshing when you drink it. If this isn't real, then you don't know what is. You mine.

Everywhere you look, you find emeralds and lapis and gold. But you've only found three diamonds so far, and you're sure there must be more, so you keep looking. Soon, your persistence pays off. You find a vein of diamonds that seems to go on forever. You start collecting them, counting as you go, but you lose count after twenty-five. You've never found so many diamonds in one spot. This is the best.

At least you think it is the best until you look up and see a Creeper. You've been so focused on mining that you didn't even notice him. You don't even have time to react before he blows up.

THE END

Going down the outside of the volcano would be deadly. And stupid. There is no way you are doing that. You and Lucky head back into the tunnel. Back into the volcano. You start down the same path you traveled earlier.

You see the crazy people, but manage to take a different path so you can completely avoid them. You don't want them near you or your dog. But they hear you and start chasing you. You and Lucky run.

You turn left then right then left again. You leave them so far behind that they will never find you. Except when you look around, it seems like you are in a tunnel with no exit. Lava flows all around you. And the worst part is that every second it grows. Pretty soon, you and Lucky can't take a step.

You wrap your arms around Lucky as the lava closes in. At least you will die together.

As your last moments come, you hear the crazy people from down the other way. Someone says, "That will make a nice sacrifice."

THE END

You may be good at fighting, but that was a lot of guardians. And anyway, there's never anything good inside underwater temples. Well, sure, you've heard rumors, but you've never found anything good. You swim back to the surface and leave the guardians far behind.

You can't find your boat at first, but then you spot it not too far away. You swim toward it and get back in. Night comes, but you're safe from the monsters out here. You ride around in your boat looking for land, but you can't seem to find it.

One day you spot an island, and you row toward it as fast as you can. You've been eating nothing but shriveled apples for the last five days, and you'd really love some meat. But the sky seems to shift as you get closer to the island, and it disappears. You don't want to admit it, but deep down you know that it was never actually really there. It was only a mirage.

You keep rowing and keep looking for land. Soon your apples run out. You never find land before you starve to death, and your skeleton floats inside the boat on the ocean forever.

THE END

74

Y ou let out a long sigh, because you know that you have to return to the witch. You promised her the Nether Wart, and you are going to be good to your word. Anyway, she didn't let you down before, even after the villagers warned you against her. They have no idea what they are talking about. She can be trusted.

Now that you have the Nether Wart, you fight more monsters on your way back to her portal. It's right where you left it, and you go through.

"I got the Nether Wart!" you exclaim, and you hand it to her. "Now I'm going back into the portal."

The witch takes the Nether Wart. "You shall be rewarded with eternal life," she says. Then she turns off the Nether portal.

You're about to ask her what she thinks she is doing, but then she kills you and turns you into a zombie. You roam the swamp, living forever, just like the witch said.

THE END

You aren't going to get distracted by shiny things. You need lava to turn into obsidian. And you need obsidian to make your portal. So you keep going, and soon you find the lava exactly where the villagers told you it would be. You get to work.

It's right by some water, so you easily turn enough of it into obsidian for your portal. You even make extra because you are always prepared. Then you build your Nether portal and go through.

You're a little woozy, but you quickly snap out of it and become alert. It's not a second too soon. Monsters attack, and you fight them, one by one, until they are all dead. But with all the fighting, you lose track of where you originally came in. That's okay. Now that you're in here, you can build another portal and, if luck is on your side, it will lead you back to the real world.

You're building your portal near a Nether fortress, but a wither skeleton attacks. You drop a bunch of obsidian into a river of lava. You kill the wither skeleton, but you're out of obsidian, and you haven't finished the portal. You know the chances of finding more obsidian here in the Nether are next to impossible, but what other choice do you have.

You wander the Nether forever, fighting monsters and looking for obsidian.

THE END

Your roller coaster will be the best! You take your time and make it perfect, planning it out and building it block by block. You test it in small pieces to make sure you've got the redstone hooked up right. Once the basic floor plan is done, you start building up. You are so careful, and you even build yourself a structure to stand on while you are working so you don't accidentally fall and die.

Finally, when you're done, you tear down your building structure and recycle the materials. The roller coaster is like nothing you've seen before. You name it THE DEMON because you think that sounds fierce and amazing.

You get on, sitting in the cart. Then you flip the switch and start it up. Your heart pounds, because you've never been this excited in your life. You don't think you've ever worked this hard on something either. You head up the first hill. It's so high you can see the top of the mountains. The wind rushes through your hair. Finally you're at the top, and down you go. Up and down and around the entire track. The thing is perfect!

You've gone around the track four times when you decide to take a break. But when you're passing by it, you can't reach the switch to flip it off. It's about three blocks too far away, and you're going way too fast. You try again on the next pass. And the next. But the ride keeps speeding up. If you jump, you are going to die. And if you don't jump, you will be stuck on here forever.

While you're trying to convince yourself to jump at the lowest point, you starve to death. THE DEMON has defeated you.

THE END

Forget the witch. You need to get home, back to the real world! You drop the Nether Wart and take off running for the portal. The portal flickers a couple times as you get closer to it, and you can almost see inside it. You're sure you see stuff you recognize. Your room. Your bed. But then it flickers and vanishes.

You try not to get upset, but you were so close. Then it appears again, about five blocks over from where it was. You run again, toward it, and this time you make it through.

The world shifts and goes a little hazy, but when your mind settles down, you look around. You are back in your own room, in the real world! You did it! You escaped from Minecraft.

But then you remember what the witch said about bad luck haunting you forever. From behind you, you hear the cackle of a witch. You're sure it's your imagination . . . isn't it?

THE END

You jump into the center of the villagers and pull out your diamond sword. "Give me your emeralds now!" you demand.

The villagers revolt. They pull out weapons and the fight begins. But you're really good with your sword. You easily defeat the first bunch around you. But more come. You fight them, too. You can do this. You can defeat them and get their emeralds.

Then one villager runs for a circle of torches. Too late you realize that the torches are surrounding a spawner. The villager breaks the torches, and skeletons appear. They shoot you with arrows. The last thought you have as you fall to the ground full of arrows is that maybe emeralds aren't so important after all.

THE END

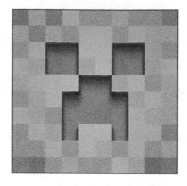

You are not the kind of person who goes back on their word. You take off the gold armor and head back toward your friends. You ran a long way, chasing the skeleton, but you made sure to remember which way you came, and soon you find them right where you originally went off on your own.

You show them the armor and tell them what happened. There is a huge amount of celebrating because they can't believe the legend was actually true either. They pass the armor around, and everyone is really happy. You are completely a hero.

Well, actually, one of your friends doesn't seem too happy. He keeps giving you dirty looks. You finally ask him what's wrong, and he admits that he wanted to be the one to find the skeleton. He tells you that it was his only goal in life. And you've ruined it.

You tell him you're sorry (even though you really aren't).

"No problem," he says, and he acts like it's all fine.

Then you split up the armor. There are four pieces of armor and five of you all. They each take a piece and then stand to leave.

"But wait," you say. "I'm the one who found it."

"Yeah, sorry about that, dude," the guy says, and then they leave you there. But not before knocking out the torches.

You try to light more torches, but they've cleaned out all your supplies. You are alone in the dark. Okay, not really alone. The monsters start to close in. Your last thought is that you never should have returned to your friends. They weren't actually your friends. But it's way too late to do anything about it

THE END

You set off to the left. The tunnel is narrow, but leads straight. Each step you take it gets narrower. You don't like narrow places, so you decide to make it a little bit wider. A small amount won't hurt.

You widen the tunnel as you go, and put up torches, and you start to feel a lot better. So much better in fact, that you get a little sloppy. You mine out one more block on your left, but it's the wrong block, and you fall into lava. It's so weird because lava shouldn't have been anywhere around here. At least that's what you thought.

THE END

Ha! Mom isn't here to tell you not to build a trampoline. You make it the biggest trampoline you possibly can power with the redstone. A small, nagging Mom voice in your head tells you that you should make it safe, too, so you build a soft barrier out of wool around it. The last thing you want to do is fall off the side and die. You can almost hear Mom saying, "I told you so."

You build a small staircase leading up to it. Then you summon the villagers so they can all come watch you. After all, you might as well open this amusement park for others. They can be visiting the slide and haunted house while you jump.

You climb the staircase and jump. Once. Twice. Twenty times. It's so much fun! And you can see everything. You do flips and splits in the air. You are an acrobat! Only after you've done every trick you know do you realize that each time you jump, you go higher. This might be a problem. You are jumping into the clouds, and they're getting your hair all wet. Next jump you'll stop.

But you don't. You bounce back, and up you go, through the clouds and through the sky barrier. You fall, but only after five feet, landing hard on your butt. It really hurts. You look at your hand. It's not blocky. Nothing is blocky anymore. That's it! You are out of the server. Out of the game. Jumping through the sky barrier did it.

You think about drinking the green potion again. But the server is full and you can't get on. Dad calls you for dinner. He will never believe what happened.

THE END

It's really tempting to leave the bunker, but you've read lots of stories about people who build bunkers. Lots of times they put traps around them to keep people away. Now that you've made it here, you are going to play it safe and live here.

Chests are filled with enough food to last ten lifetimes, and water flows into a small fountain in the bunker. The place is perfect. You craft and expand the place and make some traps of your own, to make sure nobody ever messes with you. It's a great life. Only one thing will make it better. So you make a plan.

Every so often, you put on the gold armor and you head out into the tunnels, making sure you get spotted before returning to your bunker. People think you are a skeleton wearing full gold armor. You are the new legend. You wonder if the skeleton you shot to get the armor was actually the old owner of the bunker. You guess it doesn't really matter now. You like being the new legend, and you plan to live this way for the rest of your life.

One day you are out in the tunnels, helping spread the legend of the skeleton in full gold armor when you find yourself surrounded by four people. They all fire arrows at you at the same time. Your last thought is that maybe one of them will carry on the legend after you.

THE END

You love Lucky, but not enough to give up your life in the real world. You've had time exploring, but now it is time to find a way home. You tell this to Lucky, and he seems to get upset. He runs off, down the mountain, jumping from one rock to the next, leaving you there to find a way down on your own. You're sad to see him go, but it's not like you could have taken him back to the real world.

You look down at your map to plan out the best way to go. It leads your down and around the mountain. But pretty soon it seems like it is leading you in circles. Or else you're just reading it wrong.

You check around, turning it around it case you've been holding it upside down. That's it! That was the problem. You were going the wrong way. You take a step forward because that's what the map tells you to do, and you step off a cliff.

THE END

A statue of you is way too interesting to not investigate. There are a bunch of buildings around, and you knock on a few doors until some people come out. You start to say something, and point at the statue, but the people fall to their knees before words can even come out of your mouth.

You try another building, but everywhere you go is the same. Finally you knock on a door, and manage to convince the villager to tell you what is going on.

He invites you inside, and you sit down. There, he explains that you are the creator of everything, and that is why they have a statue of you. They think of you like a king. Or maybe even like a god. It's kind of weird and kind of flattering all at the same time.

You assure the guy that you are just a normal person who likes to play video games. He has no idea what video games are, and even though you try really hard, you can't explain it to him. You try to explain about the server and how it can be turned off and on. He has no clue what you're talking about, but seems to get a little upset about the 'turning off' part. Finally you tell him that you have to go. After all, you need to get back to building your own Nether portal.

You walk to the door, but it won't open. Instead a trapdoor opens under your feet, and you fall inside.

"We can never let you leave," the guy says. "If you do, you may be unhappy with us and destroy the world. We can't let you turn us off."

You assure him that you would never do this, but he doesn't believe you. Instead he and the other villagers keep you in there forever. They tell you that this way you can never turn off the server.

THE END

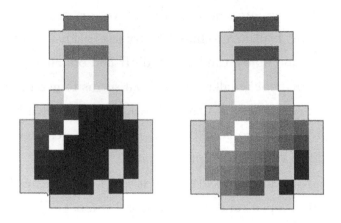

You take the tunnel to the right, because right has to be right, right? It's a lame joke, but you can't figure out any other way to decide between the two tunnels. Still, you know that right is right.

The tunnel to the right leads straight and up, not too steep, and you follow it. It's already been lined with torches by someone else. You don't see a single monster. It's almost easy. You're careful to watch out for lava and gravel and anything else that can kill you, and before you know it, you are outside!

It's daytime out. You have no idea how many days have passed. It doesn't matter. What does matter is that directly ahead of you is a building. You are sure you've seen this building before, but you can't remember when. You've played a lot of Minecraft. You walk forward and go into the building.

Inside are two chests. In one chest is a yellow potion. In the other is a green potion. Now you remember when you've seen this building before. This is the same building you entered when you got on the server. When you drank the green potion that got you into this entire mess.

If you drink the green potion because it's sure to get you out of here, turn to page 103.

If you drink the yellow potion because the green potion was a complete disaster last time, turn to page 4.

You can't leave Lucky. Not now. Not ever. Whatever food you think about, he brings it to you. You decide to stay. You build an amazing house and set up a farm and settle in to your life. You find Lucky a mate, and they have babies. The babies are really cute and love to lick your nose.

Every so often you think about your life back in the real world, but it's not enough to make you ever want to leave. But one day everything goes black. You don't know if the server got unplugged or the world got deleted or what, but it's all gone. Except you are still here. It's like your body is somehow trapped on the Internet, even though the server is gone. It's a horrible life—you just kind of exist and do nothing—but you can't find any way out.

THE END

Forget the emeralds. It's not worth getting anyone killed over. You focus instead on being a good king. You listen to the people as they come talk to you. You settle their arguments. You help them set up a farming system and learn to trade with other villages. Your kingdom grows. Word spreads about what an amazing king you are. The people love you. And you love the people.

Time goes by, and your adventurous spirit begins to come back. You've been king long enough. You gather the people and tell them that you will be going on an epic journey and that you may not come back. Maybe you shouldn't have said this last part, because the villagers start to get really worried, and when you try to pack your bag, they won't let you. So you make a run for it. You can collect new supplies outside of the kingdom. But they block the way.

"We can't let you leave," one of the villagers says. "We would kill you before we would let you go."

That is not so good. You're stuck here forever. Being king was fun at first, but now you wonder how long it will keep going on. You dream of the day someone unplugs the server, hoping it will kick you out of the game and back into the real world, but that day never seems to come.

THE END

Sure, the room could be a dungeon, but you just fought like a million guardians and the boss. You have to at least check it out. You walk into the room, and the door closes behind you. But there is plenty of air in the room, and you take off the helmet and set it down.

The room is really weird. It's not like anything you've ever seen in Minecraft before. Not like anything you and friends have ever built or come across. The walls have all sorts of screens on them, and there are controls and keyboards everywhere. One of the screens even shows the witch's hut! The pile of goo that she turned into is still out front. Another screen shows a volcano, and there's a floating island and some villagers.

This is like some sort of control room!

You sit down at one of the keyboards and type a couple quick commands. Some words pop up in a box on the screen in front of you.

MOD MINECRAFT? it says.

You get a great idea. The best idea ever. You type YES, and then you get to work. You've created mods before. Just because you are inside the game, this is no different. This control room is here for a reason. You work on your mod for about an hour, and then it's done.

You upload it to the server, and the control room vanishes. You wind up back in your room, back in the real world. And the server is still online. There's a box on the screen that says, ENTER NEW MOD?

You think about typing YES, but you decide to wait, just for a little bit. It's nice to be back in the real world. But you also wonder who is behind the server in the first place. You'll have to spend some time, maybe after dinner, investigating this.

THE END

A statue of you is really creepy. Like way too creepy. You tiptoe back in the other direction because you need to get out of here as fast as you possibly can. You hadn't noticed before because you were so focused on the statue, but there are also a bunch of buildings around. As you tiptoe away, people start to come out of the buildings.

"What are you doing here?" one of them asks. She doesn't look very happy.

You think about telling them that the statue is you, but that's just too weird, so you assure her that you were just visiting but are now leaving.

She doesn't believe you. "You were trying to destroy our statue, weren't you?" she says.

"I would never do that!" you quickly say.

But she doesn't listen. Actually none of the people listen. They turn hostile and kill you.

THE END

Y ou slam the chest closed with the yellow potion, open the chest with the green potion, and drink the green potion as fast as you can. Nothing seems to happen at first, but then the world starts to close in around you and everything goes black.

When the world returns, you blink a few times and look around. You are in your room. At home. In the real world! You did it. You actually traveled inside Minecraft and returned to tell about it. You set your controller down, and run outside. The sun warms your face and the world smells amazing. You forgot how great outside really was. There are birds and trees and best of all? There are no monsters trying to kill you. Maybe you'll take a break from video games for a while. After all, what if you'd been trapped inside Minecraft forever? That would have been horrible. And as cool as Minecraft is, the real world is a pretty cool place, too.

THE END

Sure, it is really tempting to stay in the bunker forever, but if you do that, you will never get back to the real world. It is better to keep trying than to stay safe and never get out. So you pack up what supplies you can and set out.

But whoever created the bunker didn't want anyone to ever know about it. You aren't twenty blocks away from the bunker when you step on what you think is rock but is actually gravel. You fall into a pit. Thankfully it's not a deep pit. You can build some steps and climb back out.

You light a torch so you can see what you're doing. Big mistake. The entire bottom of the pit is lined with TNT. The whole thing is a trap, built by whoever built the bunker, to keep the location secret forever. The TNT explodes, and the secret of the bunker dies with you.

THE END

Going into the room is definitely not a good idea. Underwater temples are known for dungeons, and that last thing you want to do is get locked in there and drown. After all, you aren't even sure how long the helmet will let you breathe underwater. You cast the room a final glance and head out to explore the rest of the underwater temple.

There are no more guardians, and it's almost a little spooky being down here, underwater, all alone. Everything is so quiet. You clap your hands together, but they don't make a sound. Nothing makes a sound. Not even the guardian as it swims up to you from behind. If only you'd heard it, you might have had time to get your sword out.

THE END

The more you look at the soul sand, the more you can't ignore it. Each soul looks like a person, and if there really are souls trapped inside, maybe you can help them. Then you can decide what to do about the portal. You pull out a potion and throw it at the soul sand. Something tells you that it is the right one. And then you wait.

Slowly souls begin to rise from the sand. They're like ghosts at first, but then they materialize and become real people just like you.

"You freed us," one of them says. It looks really strange when he opens his mouth, but you aren't sure why.

Then all of them open their mouths and expose horrible fangs. They lunge at you and drag you down, into the sand. There they trap your soul forever.

THE END

A NOTE FROM CONNOR

To all the Gamers out there:

Thank you so much for taking the time to read *Pick Your Own Quest: Escape from Minecraft*! It's gamers (and readers) like you who will create the future of games!

If you did enjoy reading *Pick Your Own Quest: Escape from Minecraft*, I would love if you would take a few moments to review the book on Amazon. Reviews are so important these days, and even a one sentence review can make a huge difference in other readers discovering the series.

Now go and play some more games (or read another book)!

—CONNOR HOOVER

A NEW MYTHOLOGY SERIES
PERFECT FOR RICK RIORDAN
FANS!

LOOK FOR

A SERIES BY
CONNOR HOOVER!

LIKE VIDEO GAMES?
THINK MAGIC AND MONSTERS
ARE COOL?

LOOK FOR

A SERIES BY
CONNOR HOOVER!

LIKE ADVENTURE STORIES?
THINK ALIENS ARE COOL?

LOOK FOR

A SERIES BY
CONNOR HOOVER!

LOOK FOR

Ancient Egypt is in serious trouble…

Crazy things are happening in Egypt! The gods are angry. The Nile River is drying up. Smoke appears on the horizon. Crocodiles attack! It's up to you to save the world. Make the right choice and you get to rule Egypt for the rest of your life. Make the wrong choice and it will be your last.

Remember, you can't turn back. Sorry! Once you make a choice, it can't be changed.

CHOOSE WISELY :)

ABOUT THE AUTHOR

If Connor Hoover had to pick one potion to drink, it would be blue because it's Connor's favorite color. Also, it might give Connor the ability to breathe underwater, and then Connor could explore ocean monuments. Connor lives in Austin, Texas and has a video game machine with 410 retro video games including Ms. Pac-Man, Frogger, and Connor's personal favorite Q*bert.

To contact Connor:

connor@connorhoover.com

www.connorhoover.com